Gray hound traveling with Jeff Bozorth, And High Frequency Communication.

Part one.

When I was working at a cereal Plant near Dillion Mt, I started hearing a lot of voices in my head. I also audible heard a lot of voices in my head when I was working at the plant trying to do my shift. Some of the guys I was working with Jason and Camron were also messing with me because they could tell I was schitzoing out. I had a guy I grew up with come into town and was yelling outside my apartment saying some bad rumors about me. messing with me also told me to stick up for myself. I also started yelling at him. Outside my apartment they also said that my friend had killed himself so I went back to billings to check up on him. When I was in Billings I told my old roommate what I heard and sat posted up by the door on a couch with a pistol waiting for people to break in. They started shooting off guns to scare me. Then I went back to Dillon the next day. Didn't sleep and got back to work that night. I heard some weird stuff about my ex girlfriend being kidnapped. So that night I went to work and heard a multitude of voices in my head. By this time I had my guns with me. After I did my shift at work , Bo a guy that trained me to be a bagger said (Name removed) had shot himself and this was a guy that was spreading rumors about me. Shit kind of freaked me out because I thought It was I guy I had a problem with at the moose bar and almost got into a fight with him and few of his friends I needed some Dillon guys to back me up . I thought this though because there was 3 of them. I went home sad and lifted weights maybe smoked some pot? I walked back to the bar to fight because those guys hurt my feelings. Then the cops showed up at the moose and arrested those guys for disorderly because they were acting a fool at the office bar.

I went out to my car after work and had a flat tire. Which I thought that dude outside my apartment in dillion had flattened my tire. When I was at work at the plant hearing the voices of the people I thought were grouping up outside my work. Then I went back home and told my parents I was leaving and or called them.

There was a big snow storm. I went driving on my doughnut on my car. To butte and got some sleep in my car at rest stop for about an hour or two till I saw a city worker in a big city plow truck. Also thought a saw a black gang banger at the gas station, that I thought was one of the guys that jumped me back at JD's back in Billings, when that place was still open. I drove to Missoula and heard a lot of voices coming from my car, This was after my I pod was plugged in, due to my motor head saw blade shaped cd had broken my cd player. But the aux still worked so I was using my I pod but it didn't have the power to bump my speakers like the deck did. I started yelling back at the voices in the car when I was in Missoula. Then I went back through the Idaho and I could hear the cops in my car talking about me. I could also hear the guy I grew up with constantly saying Jeff's stupid, there was also a high frequency voice frequently sticking up for me saying Jeff's smart. When I was of the road, I thought people were trying to get me

caught up in some dirt. I knew there a was a wiretap or some kind of speaker In my car or tape playing so I grabbed the glove box and ripped the bottom out of it doing this I cut my arm a little bit gripped the wires looking for the problem I thought I had some kind of tape or listening device I threw out of my car window when I was driving it kind of dimmed the head lights. It was night by this time, and I was over by Hamilton, MT. I went to my parents' house and tried to get my daughter and leave town. They called the cops on me partly because I said some strange accusations to my parents that the guy messing with me had said to me.

Some thing he said was that my mom was poisoning me and had wrote a life story about me. This is when I left alone for my folk's house and went to the hospital and checked on my daughter's mom because I thought my something bad had happened to her. From some of the voices I was hearing from my neighbors at my apartment complex. I thought she had been raped or kidnapped or something so I had them do a welfare check up on her and her son trey, that I had help raise with my daughter when I lived in billings. So at the Dillon hospital they said they would check on her I went to leave I was walking to my car and the cops showed up, my parents called them on me, they detained me back at the hospital and did a check up on me. They also found my guns in my car a Ak47 and a 38cal sitting on my passenger seat. Found I had a super-fast heart rate and small traces of weed in my system. Then they held me there till morning and took me to warm springs State Hospital. The same cop that had tried to bust me for weed when I was speeding to work at the cereal plant.

They checked me into warm springs, and I was put in room 14. Frank Costello told me you hear that? That's Obama hovering above warm springs in a helicopter. He said good job to me. Went I went into my room I heard a guy with a radio in the next room and it sounded like Obama was talking about me in a speech also heard young buck rapping about me. I also heard some people chanting free Jeff Bozorth. I thought Obama was going to pardon me. It never happened. So, I spent about 5 months in warm springs lifting weights and reading. I stopped a girl breaking the tv in the tv room with a chair. I watched her break it the sturdy plastic around the tv with the chair till she got to the tv its self and then I got up and grabbed the chair and held it till the staff went in there. It seems that I helped the patients chill out more that the psychiatrists. I also had a few friends in there that I hung out with. I would work out 2 or 3 times a day most of the time. I had a girl that was kind of like a girlfriend that had yellow skin but was very pretty. She used to be a stripper at the Alaskan bush company and had bit a guard In the billings woman's jail. There was also a girl from Hamilton that said I was different from everybody else in there. She also showed me her vagina. Another girl looked like jades' cousin a big native girl that was constantly in there. She would also fool around with frank. One the guys supposedly got busted with a knife unless the guy that found it planted it. He got put in jail after that he was in there because he said a native raped him in great falls to get back at him for having sex with his girlfriend and the cops busted him with a bat with nails in it. One of my other friends was from Missoula and got in trouble for robbing a convenience store. But he didn't tell me that. I admired a counselor named Jesse from L.A a big white dude with tattoos, he was relatable and a nice guy, he said what is your favorite show Hawaii 50 I started laughing.

Because he knew something about me fighting with the Hawaiians' that lived next door to me. His dad had a heroin problem and would prefer to date black ladies. He told us about getting in to a fight in jail because someone stole his ice cream. Jesse later died from a heart attack. Before I got a job cleaning the gym there and worked into a job in the kitchen washing dishes, one of the longer sentence guys was jealous of me because of some of the rumors about me.

When I got out, I was getting big from working out all the time. My parent came and picked me up and we went to the Montana club for breakfast in butte on the way home. I went home and smoked for a while on the rest of the once I had locked up in a chest. I spent a year at my parents' house depressed and not feeling that good about myself partly because of the some of the harsh rumors going on about me. I Finally got a job that summer doing hay in the ruby ranch on the Hershey's land. I drove my truck over there and I thought It was wire tapped. I kept singing that I love you Mary jane song. It was in the big hole valley. I thought I could her aliens communicating with me from the fridge in the bunk house. I drove a scatter rake to start I got It stuck in a ditch because I thought that was we're I thought I was supposed to cross the irrigation ditch at and got it stuck on a fence also. Some of the kids working there had a bong in their bunk house I hit it. A kid also had some weed he smoked with me on a tractor when we we're doing beaver slides. They had their meals cooked for them, so they did not make as much as us guys working at the ruby. My bunk mate and I started off ok but started not to like each other. I went back to Dillon for my daughter birthday and for getting some groceries. When I got back to the Ruby ranch my macaroni and cheese and beer was gone I told the ranch supervisor that I was going to beat my bunk mates ass when he comes back that same guy almost got stabbed by a Mexican that stayed next door to us. When I was in Dillon visiting my family. He got let go when he came back.

 One night I heard some guys surround my bunk house and said are you saying you part of our biker club and I said I'm not saying that shit to anybody people just started saying that about me. They said you're a rat if you drive a truck with a wiretap in it. The Mexican's next door I wonder If they heard voices coming from my truck because when I told them about the wiretap, they said you better get a good lawyer. Some of the shift I would get a feeling of aliens watching me in the tractor, on like an alien T.V. show that I was a big star on their T.V. show. One of the last days when I was driving the tractor, I thought there was an arm in the gas tank it because I could smell something strange burning when I was driving it. I did not really feel safe after that and felt like I needed some guns, so I went back to Dillon. Which sucked because I almost did the whole season, but I missed the $500-dollar bonus because I left early only about 2 days. Might off been a good thing because a few years earlier a Mexican guy died there at the end of the season because he had his load up too high in the air when he went down a big ass hill in a tractor that had no cab and it rolled over on him. I went back to talk to the boss lady landowner and tried to get paid but she said she would send me a check and I gave her my address. After working at the ruby, I pretty much left town right away and tried to get some guns. I went over to my brother's house in Bozeman and it seemed I was getting followed by some bikers that were hooting and hollering in my brother's neighborhood. When I was laying down trying to get some sleep I could her a weird power full Wa Wa Wa sound in his block that sounded like a UFO sending a strong signal or hovering. Aliens seemed to be mad that everybody was messing with me. I can't remember what they said. I think they did say something. After that I left and started driving to Salt Lake City, I saw some stars in the sky that UFO. On the road to big sky and I went to a hotel to get directions to Salt Lake City where I was planning to live. I drove to Idaho through the southern highway out of Big sky. When I got to Idaho falls, I got a hotel and tried to get some sleep, in one of the adjacent rooms I heard what I thought was a fed talking about me getting messages from aliens. I did not feel safe, so I got in my car after staying there for a about an hour or a half hour. Started driving I could hear my loose change vibrating in a indention above the stick shift and it seemed to be aliens communicating with me, they told me to make peace with Obama also warned the feds to leave me alone. They said that they liked me the vibrations were strong, so it seemed that they were angry, this was in Idaho driving in the early morning. I went to a gas station. Then went to Salt Lake. Went to Salt Lake airport and got a ticket to Washington Dc for about a thousand dollars. This where I might of talked about the yakuza's were using Japanize technology to edit wire recording from wire taps and falsely incriminate people with voice cuts with the dialog of people talking after the feds had it recorded. And that the government was kidnapping American girls for the Chinese to take to china to be sex slaves to pay off the debt. This kidnapping thought is most likely a schizoid thought I no longer believe. The wiretap thought or radio signal I believe our government has the technology to do that them self's most likely.

When I was in the plane going to D.C. I heard an older gray haired white guy with a hat and black guy in his 20's talking and they were talking about me being the next president and some other guys I don't remember were talking about me in a negative light. I could hear a strong humming signal and weird looking storm, massive grey clouds all around the city storming and lightning when I got to DC. I asked a young Asian guy in the seat in front of me for his phone so I could call my family I tried and from what I remember I don't think it worked.

I arrived at the airport in DC and got a phone card to call my family and they said that my daughter was next door playing with the neighbor's daughter and I was mad because I had some bad thoughts about the police man next door to my parents' house due to the speaker and or wiretap in my car, I heard someone say that he had naked pictures of my baby's mom, so that had led me to believe some pretty strange stuff about him. There was a strange vibe in the airport, and I heard people saying that the president had killed himself. When I stepped out the massive airport, I looked at the road that runs right by the taxi pick up's spot at the airport and saw the presidential motor cade going by with a big black limo with tinted windows and people said "see he didn't kill himself". I struggled a while to get a cab and when I finally did the driver was of Indian or middle eastern descent, he asked me where I was going I told him that I would stay in the cheapest hotel that was in D.C. "The Americana is the cheapest motel in D.C." I told him to take me there then. He then asked me what my business was in D.C I said I was there to meet with the president. The cab driver then mentioned that there were tours to the white house, but I seemed unlikely that I was going to meet with the president without official business. After a bit we reached the Americana hotel which had at a many massive rows of bikes which were Harley's or Harley type bikes. Walking inside I saw a small lobby and went upstairs. I went into my room and tried to get some sleep. There were some interesting people in their 2 younger guys in there early 20's stayed near to my room they seemed to be meeting someone at the white house I thought they were slandering me, there was also an slightly overweight man about 5'5 that seemed to be watching me, possibly working for the pentagon I had some strange thoughts about the bikers outside that they had a hit list and killed the guy that had me on it, I believe was one of the thoughts. Going down into the lobby there was a guy with a beard on a laptop that seemed interesting to me, like he was a fellow psychic with powers like myself. I thought that I was a sitting duck in the hotel, so I decided to go to Pittsburg because since I was in grade or middle school, I've been a Pittsburg Steelers fan. I then called a cab to pick me up and I think I lost my $100 dollars I paid for the room. I called a cab and then left the hotel. The cab driver seemed cool and I looked outside the window at the big city life on the way to the bus station and saw some hookers. The big overweight cab driver who seemed jolly with some mirth said yeah you mess with these girls and you'll get aids, I agreed. After a bit I arrived at the greyhound station paid the cabdriver and got inside.

I am from Montana, so it seemed like there were a lot of black people inside compared to what I'm used to, maybe one or two other white people it seemed like. A black dude around my age at that time about 27 asked me if I needed anything said "man let's get out of here and get some pussy" I replied to him and said "nah man I'm good", It seemed a lot like a set up for a robbery or a mugging. One of the other white older dudes in his 40's or early 50's, wearing a yellow shirt seemed to be working for the feds or someone else seemed to be talking into his neck. On the tv in the bus station the tv started to say that the president had killed himself and told me it was my fault and to kill myself and no one had seen him in a few days or a week. The TV had a news caster on there and it kept telling me to kill myself.   Which tripped me out and thought Obama had been involved In jades disappearance (the people at the hospital in Dillon did a welfare check on her I believed and she was ok) so I said some bad things about Obama, Some older black guy said and that "fucker didn't even eat a breath mint". Another guy that seemed to be a police man or undercover detective to me yelled "this fuckers got problems with Obama" and was announcing it to the whole bus station when I got on a bus to Pittsburg he said "oh he's going to Pittsburg, that where he is going" he said it very loud. I got on the bus it seemed like I was one of the only people on the bus. The bus driver and his crony which were middle aged black guys seemed to be pissed off at me and were talking about dropping me off in a bad neighborhood to get shanked or beat up by some gangbangers. When I got to a town close to Pittsburg it seemed like everybody knew who I was. A Mexican guy seemed like a veteran or ex-service member said some Facebook rumors and a couple of women did the same thing. He said you better not be going to the burg or something to that effect. There was a drag queen or a manly looking lady that was sticking up for me saying "if he said that about me, I would whoop his ass". It seemed like all the buses were wire tapped and some Mexican girls behind me acted strange. A younger black guy got on and a drunk hillbilly type got in the seat in front of me that looked like a relative to the asshole on the plane ride. When we got close to Pittsburg another Mexican 20 or so years old guy a bit bigger in the belly kept making a explosion noises with his mouth. The young black collage looking guy that recently got on the bus said stick up for yourself and I said in the bus "it wasn't me it was this guy" gesturing to the drunken hillbilly type guy in the bus seat in front of mine. When I arrived at Pittsburg, I went to the army navy store and bought a green army backpack, some nice pants and a knife. When in the store it seemed like the store owner or worker had been told to tell me to be a state informant for the cops that I had till the 18 of September (I don't remember the exact day I wrote down the 18th of September not too sure). Then I walked to a famous deli by the bus station. When I got to the deli, I got a sandwich and a man in a black suit walked into the left of me and too the right behind me was a table with four middle aged guys with sandwiches. They said "I hope he goes somewhere nice not New York I hate new York and acted like Jeremy smith was abducted by a UFO outside the apartment complex, talking about lights similar to Christmas lights picking him and acted like they had saved my life a whole bunch of times. When I finished my sandwich, I got up and said if you want to check out something checkout the wire tap's in the airplane going to Ohio, it was a side flight to dc. The fed sitting behind me said a bunch of horrible stuff about shooting my ex-girlfriend and shooting people and seemed like he was trying to get me to say something to incriminate myself, then acted like they were playing a game him and a women and a man with a ball of paper saying shoot it over here. When the plane about landed or landed he said loudly do you know how many man hours of sentencing I've been a part of. I thought they might possibly be hitman that were going to take me out once I was walking around.

Any way back to the sandwich shop it was a pretty good sandwich and fries. That is when I got lost and was looking around the area of the Pittsburg greyhound for hours then It seemed that the crowds of people were against me and people on Facebook or involved with the government were gossiping about me. And it seemed like some of the groups of city people were out to get me. I wrote down that people were yelling about me. So, I started walking down alleys instead of streets, I walked into a club and they told me that I needed a drink to hang out there. Then I kept walking up and down a market place until I got tired of it and asked for some directions to the greyhound.

When I got there, I saw some out of place teen age or 20 something year old black guys that I thought were working for Obama. They were acting pretty shady and after a while I noticed that the wire taps in the bus station were linked to the radio station that was playing in the bus stop and were saying something about an old child hood friend of mine, Ike getting corn holed and that he was found underneath Jeff's truck seemingly like he had gotten run over. Then Obamas voice was on the radio or bus station speakers saying you need to stick up for yourself. I got more and more angry he said I was "a homosexual" and I said "fuck you" partially because I knew it wasn't true and part because It was going on the radio and also said "that's bullshit". Then I started grandstanding about Obama saying bad things about him, In the middle of the Pittsburg bus station. They also played a song about Obama getting assassinated by a group. It was sung by Beyoncé or Rihanna. And that I was a part of that group. I met a few guys about my age I told them about how everything was wiretapped and that I went to Washington D.C to talk about it and Obama didn't meet with me he just spread a bunch of rumors about me and about got me shot in Pittsburg. This small Latin guy 110 pounds,5'1 said "yeah fuck Obama".

I bought a sandwich at the deli and gave half of it to another Spanish guy that was pretty like my body type. The radio jockey on the radio said some bad things about me sleeping next door to my daughters' room in Dillon and I said your trying to ruin me "fuck you radio faggots" Then I later called them punks because there were little kids around. Then Someone said if you keep sticking up for yourself and your going to get a life sentence. Then I started standing in different bus lines to throw people off my trail. After that I believe I went and found out that I missed my bus it almost felt like something was inside me making me do that. Then I went outside the bus station where there were people outside smoking. I saw a car with Montana plates full of what looked like Asians.

It started to get dark and I hailed a cab a big stocky white guy with a bald head was driving it. He asked where I was going, and I told him that I was going to get a hotel. So, he took me to the Marriott hotel. I tried to get a room at the desk, the lady working informed me that they had no vacancy. Then I went to the bar. It seems there was another table of feds in the bar dining area. I sat at the bar with my backpack. There was a big group of huge white guys at the bar drinking I few spaces down from me on my left. While sitting there I drank four beers, there was a girl in there that was a little short and attractive she came on to me but had two guys with her. I went outside and saw some kids getting ready for a prom kind of event with some formal gear dresses and such. I decided to head out the building and go back to the grey hound. I had a strange radio frequency or telekinetic or just plain schizophrenic message that I was the secretary of defense. People seemed to be nicer to me on the streets, I remember hitting on some girls that were hot that I saw driving by then I made it back to the greyhound. When I reached the grey hound. I felt strange and I starting telling some of the black guys outside the greyhound that President Obama was in a UFO and had dropped a nuked the state of Florida and it disappeared from a vison that I had. I had these things called power statements and I could make changes to fix the universe. So, I supposedly made a power statement and brought it back. I told the black guys "I'm tired of cleaning up Obama's mistakes". The black dude that was about me age responded. "you need to take your meds"

I got a bit of a head ache and walked up the street to the train station walked upstairs close to the train tracks on the platform laid down and saw an older black dude and I looked at him like shit what now kind of spooked "He said get some sleep" and then I went to sleep in the train station because I had felt like he was going to be looking out for me. After sleeping in the train station, I walked down and the group the red hats they said so what if Obama did that stuff you're a snitch and a bunch of perverted stuff. I don't think the radio guy was still playing in the speakers any more. I walked back to the bus station and got a bus going back to Washington D.C. They said something about giving me a life sentence and the aliens said they would blow up any jail that I was in. And when we were traveling there was a big black bag that I thought

was a bomb placed in there to blow me up when everybody had got off the bus. And an older black guy picked it up and took it inside. Somewhere along this road at a stop in the crowded bathroom a big black dude offered me some powder it looked like he was snorting it on a mirror, I respectfully declined. When I got to the Washington dc bus station, I went to Marriott which was about 200 dollars a night it was genuinely nice about the nicest place I have ever stayed. I drank 3 beers Budweiser's from an older Asian woman bartender then went up to my room. Heard some strong radio signals and humming frequency and laid down to bed. I caught a cab to the D.C airport in the morning and told them that I was going back to Salt Lake City. Then at the ticket terminal I saw a very attractive black lady I saw a girl with brown eyes turn yellow when she was looking at the screen of fight info.
At the security booth I had my don't tread on me t shirt on and this big black security guard said "now that's Gangster" that was cool when I was sitting there in the airport and saw a silver cylindrical ship shaped like a sideways tear drop and it shot a pulse laser into the building and flew up in the air and back down very fast and agile. Making a 90 degree or right angle and back down shooting a what look like a rail gun or pulse type laser weapon into the front of the white house that I could see from the airport window. I believe this to be an aggressive species of alien. In the airport I made hand gestures of what I saw mimicking the movements with my hands and said wasn't that cool whoosh like I was a big kid. They someone had said while I was sitting there that they had turned the metal detectors off.
I saw what looked to be Michelle Obama right before I had boarded the plane to Salt lake city while I was wearing my yellow "don't tread on me shirt with a snake on the cover".
Which was the same design as the flag at the standoff in Oregon which happened 2016.

Then I flew to Salt Lake City I checked the underside of the car with a flashlight for bombs. Then I drove south to California and I went through Nevada I hit either a wolf or a big coyote 'smack' in the left side of the front bumper and busted out the left blinker panel, it was just sitting there in the middle of the road. I drove some more till I got to a gas station and covered it up with some reflective tape. Looking up in the sky while I was driving, I saw thousands of white streaks in the sky above me UFO, meteors or cosmic particles, for quite a while. I went to Sacramento to get my name changed but they wanted me to be a resident, and I had to put my knife and metal objects outside the building so it wouldn't set off the metal detectors. I lost where I had parked my car and had to ask a cop for help, they helped me find it after about a half an hour in the heat walking around looking at parking lots.

I started to hear songs about me one of them was called Jeffrey bomber and I think it was written by Prince, I also heard a song about a devil president a Mexican song on the radio. When I was driving in southern California close to the Mexican border. Then I could hear in my head that I had enemies in Mexico and that I shouldn't drive down there, I also heard that the only way I would get in Mexico would be a bus, and another voice said for me to make peace with my enemies by going down to Mexico.
I heard in my head that the cop that had helped me find my car was killed in L.A for snitching on me to corrupt government people telling them what my car looked like and the plates. I almost

got on a bus to go to Mexico I think I was in L.A because there were buildings with murals and a lot of Mexican people where in the town I was at. I decided not to go to Mexico and drove north to look for Arnold Schwarznegger's house, I couldn't find it and thought I heard that he had offed himself. Around that area I saw a white bottle top looking UFO in the sky and the words on the radio stations started to switch around. It looked like it was just hovering there, and I thought them to be a peaceful species of aliens I thought these might be the peaceful aliens that wanted me to make peace with Obama. I figured the craft to be hovering 50-100 stories in the air.

I headed farther north up around Fresno I believe north to where there is tomato fields and I got lost and this Is when I heard some strange noises coming from the radio. They told me some strange stuff like that Obama was an evil space alien and the head of a race of Obama's that were strange, minded aliens. Then was an evil voice that said they were going to destroy earth and I seemed like fighter jets were attacking him and one said "he is hot clam chowder" over the pacific but it seemed like he was respawning. Not long after that I made another so called power statement bring back the old good fighters of the universe then I tried to telekinetically get them to destroy the Obama's home planet that was sending bad signal's to earth.

Then I drove on a back road and went to some more tomato field and It seemed like I was following my radio signals talking to the aliens, they said "do you want to see our ship?"
I looked and I saw a ship on the ground that looked like it was having problems with gravity these seemed like some nomadic traveling type of aliens. They said "look at our new ship isn't it cool" and I said yeah and waved at them then they got airborne and flew directly right over my car I saw them approach and I got scared. They had a huge black craft with light horizontally bordering the center. Then I went to a gas station after I was all pumped up and lost and got gas and told them (the people working) that there might be some valuable stuff in a field. I went back out with my flashlight and searched around. They had big tomato harvesting machines running it looked like they were digging up UFO scraps because of the UFO battle. Then I went back to the car. I Noticed a lot of semi-trucks parked by the side of the road my assumption was for UFO scrap parts. I heard something I my head say that I was the only one with permission to be looking for UFO space material out in the fields.

Then I drove south so I could go east but got trapped between highways and took a rest in my car. I got up when there was some sunlight then kept driving past the blocked off highway sign until I heard a voice saying that "their trying to trick you" and I went down the blocked exit ramp that had cones and finally made it on the right highway. After getting on the right road I went north east to Reno I got there and parked in a parking garage and went inside the airport with my hat tilted to the side and my sunglasses on and heard in a message in my mind that I had a ticket waiting for me to go to japan and I kept checking different airline counters for it. Finally, one of the people working in the airport called the cops on me. I went outside and a talked to the cops I told them about an airplane being scrambled to blow up my parents' house and a UFO blowing it up. I actually managed to get my licenses back from the police after telling him I was travelling and that was my only id.

Then I left the airport got in my car and drove it out of the car garage, the la cucaracha, started driving north and kept getting on the California national forest road two or three time and was scared that crooked government officials were coming after me trying to kill me. While in my car I heard the radio do some strange things like an evil impersonation of Obama saying he was going to cut my balls off with his space knife and rip my face off and he sounded like the devil. Then I went to burger king and got a hamburger and some chicken strips at pueblo I think and finally went through the forest road back to Reno. Then went north up through Nevada till the wiretap told me to get off the road the evil Obama space ship was after me and I went to the love lock hotel and casino. I had a few beers and some women at the desk told me to get up at 6.

The evil space alien told me in my head that he would have zapped me if I was still driving around. There was a nice married woman that was decent looking that wanted to walk me to my room, but I told her no, that she was married, and she seemed a bit drunk. I couldn't find my room and ended up getting help from a maintenance guy found it went inside and took a bath then went to bed. When I woke up a guy drove up and asked me for money, I felt paranoid, so I left the car and went with the panhandling guy who was driving an older SUV. I told him I would give him money if he drove me to Pittsburg. I told him about aliens and scared him because he asked if I had any weapons on me and I said I had a knife in my bag , I also asked him If he wanted a joint and he said no. He pretty much ripped me off and didn't give me a very far ride I put 40$ dollars in his tank and gave him a hundred because I thought he was going to give me a ride to Pittsburg. When on the way to a bus stop, he would be panhandling truckers asking them for dollars and told him that he was riding with Jesus because I was a while guy with a beard in his SUV. Then he dropped me off at the bus stop I got a ticket and waited outside until the bus came and I had a stop in Salt Lake City. Think at this point a went to Salt Lake and then later to Denver.

Salt lake city when I arrived here I decided to walk and get some food I strolled through a drug infested area where people were shooting up with syringes and asked me if I wanted any drugs, I said no and continued walking to mc Donald's. Saw an attractive 22-year-old girl and talked to her and her friend for a little while she was a short dark skinned and skinny and her friend was white and about the same youthful look just a little bit older. A guy gave me a cheeseburger and I ate it because the lobby was closed, I went to a gas station and saw a bunch of black guys playing rap music. I went outside and sat down for a while, before I had reached that store UI saw a Mexican guy arguing with a hot Asian girl and told him to stop yelling at here this almost caused a fight. Then I walked downtown to a park with a lot of homeless people congregating I slept away from the main homeless population in the park and got up and walked toward the grey hound and a group of young black guys tried to sell me some drugs. I said no I asked where the greyhound was, and he replied do you have some money? I gave him a dollar or a five and walked to the grey hound with my new directions. When I got to the grey hound in salt lake I went to the bathroom and took a diarrhea dump my insides hurt from that cheese burger and I thought I got a psychic signal that he was shot for poisoning me and that the defense dept. had him give me the poisoned burger.

 While in Denver I glanced into the window and It looked like my face was changing into the face of Jesus Christ's with balding long hair. I met up with a older white convict outside the bus stop and went downtown Denver with him (he knew I was from out of town and wanted to show me the town) and checked out the live music and mall street I got a bacon burger and checked out the subway transportation. Or bus station not too sure now . On one of the rail cars on Mall street, there was a black guy mean mugging me and he got off when I did. Psychic signals went out of my brain after I was resting on a bench outside of a bar and I think they heard noises from hell on their tv sets. There was also a person that took a picture of me while I was laying down.
I sent out a strong telepathic message "Don't mess with Heasus" and later was told in my mind that the message was reverberating far off distant planets. I talked to a homeless guy that looked like a beat up easy-e and gave him a dollar he was trying to sell me some DVD and was talking about us going to try to get some pussy I don't think that would have been very quality pussy at all. He was talking about that fact that the real gangsters work and live in the big sky rises in Denver.
Later on after that I went into to a different part of town and say a drunk girl walking around, a pretty cute blond about 5'5 160 and followed her until some other people a couple watched out for her for me. Then I made it back to the bus stop. On the way saw ambulances and thought it might be because of my telekinesis that some people in the city were getting hurt. I saw some police men and they looked angry with me.
At the bus stop there was a black dude about late 30's or early 40's that seemed kind of like a hustler. His women left or the girl he was messing with and wanted me to help him go through her bag he said "hey big Jeff lets go through this stuff" "I said let's see if there are any bombs in it".
I believe I slept that night at the grey hound in Denver and the next morning I saw jades ex-boyfriend jimmy and his dad. At the Denver bus stop, they probably thought that I was still with jade but I wasn't I thought that she had been murdered they thought the same I believe and they thought that I had something to do with it.

So I went on the bus to St. Louis It seemed like the older Mexican guy that was with jimmy was talking shit about me walking home from the moose but not about the fact that I went back to the moose to fight after I walked home. He seemed scared and ran outside the bus or bus stop and it seemed like he got shot or shot in the head by a proton particle plasma beam at least it seemed that way because the St louis cop were pissed off at me and looking at me and I started laughing. He was a short older looking Mexican. The cop was a black guy he seemed angry at me and couldn't charge me for hurting the guy. They were supposedly going to arrest him for slander or stalking.
Then I walked to market street and went to the 711 and got a jug of water(which is what I drank a lot of with bags of mixed nuts)a guy came in he was a older man and he seemed

worried or scared and seemed to be working with the government or the police. I left the store and went to look around the park I sat down on a park bench. While I was sitting there a beat up older looking white dude was talking about a black guy at the store took some money or something from him and that he was going to get his brother and fuck him up and called the guy a nigger I said when his brother got there he was going to go after the black guy who robbed him. A group of bloods started walking down the road and were yelling while they walked down the street to the park "Jeffery Jeffery" they walked up to us I sat there for a minute and we were just looking at each other. I decided to leave and walked back to the gray hound station. While I was walking down to the bus station, I saw a scary looking black dude that looked like Obama's evil dropple ganger and he seemed mad as hell. He was talking to some cab drivers or cops or someone. There was a big heavy set black guy outside trying to get me to buy some cd's and I told him no I didn't want any that I didn't know what was on the cd's and he could be trying to set me up. I guess he asked this puck ass looking white dude some coke and that white guy snitched on him to the metro cops so they went up to me and asked if I was offered to buy drugs and "I told them no he was just trying to sell me cd's" I saw I girl laying down in the grey hound with a blanket and she looked like one of my past girlfriends I was worried that something bad happened to her because of the people the hate me.

I took the greyhound then to the Pittsburg area while it was sitting there I had my knife pulled out and waiting for someone to come after me in the bus. I also saw a Asian guy with his mom and I said I don't have any problem with Asians as long as they don't kidnap people. Then I went to Pittsburg on the bus and when I arrived in the bus station I was kind of out of it and walked into a office type area and it pissed this big black dude off he kept saying "where's your ticket" get out of here. While in the bus station I saw a Chinese man with his son I talked to him about drinking beer and also talked to a Iranian man from Iran and talked to him and said "you're from Iran that's cool". This older white dude and I were talking and I told him I was going to Philadelphia and he said filthadelphia.

At around this point I think the big black gray hound worker kicked me out of the bus station. I then took a cab to the motel 6 in Pittsburg I thought Obama was after me at this point and that the owner of the Pittsburg Steelers started a private investigator detective agency and gave it to jimmy. I think this white tough guy looking dude was following me and was also hoping for a job at the private detective agency. There were young black guys with suits that I also thought they were working for the detective agency. This pissed the tough looking white dude off and thought that they gave our jobs away. This white dude was on the bus with me when we were going through Kansas City.
I walked though Pittsburg in the morning through a black neighborhood and got a sandwich at subway they seemed to not like me outside the subway sandwich shop I heard a crows saying "hey big jeff" Some white dudes in a car were saying "I hate this neighborhood to many niggers" While at Pittsburg train station while I was waiting for a ticket to Philadelphia a guy

walked in that looked like a homeland security officer he was official looking agent with a suit and I seemed like he was trying to put me in jail for talking bad about the president Obama. A middle aged bald white guy helped me out and I told him I needed a knife he said "Naw man you don't need any knifes" While I was at the train station I saw two young guys kind of crying saying lets send this "stuff to this family so they don't think he was dead" putting some stuff in a box acting weird. I don't think they were talking about me. I stayed the night in the train station and then left on the train to Philadelphia.

On the Amtrak to Philadelphia I heard people messing with armrests and I thought they were cocking pistols and that some people behind me in the train were messing with me. This greyhound bus driver Curtis had had me recorded on tapes that he kept putting In I thought I psychic told him my life story and it got recorded on the tapes on one of my trips back to Pittsburg. In Philly I got a passport photo and went to the passport office and tried to get my passport I think they told me I would have to wait a week. I then walked through town and got a water from some black dude selling water and I was kind of lost saw a pimp walking down the sidewalk and he gave me a dirty look. It seemed like I was getting bad transmissions or signals in my head and had to sit by an old big church to chill out it seemed like that help my head frequencies to settle down. I got a cab and a African man said that you have a powerful demon inside of you. I went to the Philadelphia grey hound station I saw a black dude and he was asking for money to get a bus ticket home he busted out a bag of weed and asked if I wanted to buy it, it looked decent but I was on a Jesus trip and not smoking and not heavy drinking, I gave him the 10 or 15 dollars he asked for and he was very thankful he said that I should came down and hang out with him and his family(I didn't take the weed).

When I walked into the grey hound in Philadelphia and sat down I seemed to project Curtis the bus drivers voice out of me saying his spiel about what he would say about arriving to Pittsburg and that his dad was a cop it seemed to trip out some of the black people waiting for the bus that I thought knew Curtis. A black security guard seemed to hate me. After I was sitting there watching tv for a while I saw the news and the dude I gave the ten dollars was on there and said that he had to be Jesus that gave him the money for his bus ticket and that he was going fishing. I decided against taking to bus because I thought people were coming after me and I decided to take a cab to the airport.

While I was in the cab on the way to the airport a Ukrainian cab driver said that if I misuse my power the portal will open that night was strange and people were lying to me saying that I was going to be inaugurated and after that a bunch of people were walking around in a panicky saying things like "the worlds going to end" I told them it's not just calm down and there was some maintenance guys there and some homeland security guys talking and I telepathically told asked him which side he was on I and that I have powers and could be a important person in a foreign country. And I could get them jobs there. At the Philadelphia airport I got a ticket to

Bismarck but through the signals and what seemed like the intercom I kept looking for my passport to japan till I lost track of time and missed my flight.

They had just got done waxing a part of the floor and I had been upstairs and went down there and there was some hubbub about inaugurating me and after the Pittsburg bus incident there was an older lady from Africa and she seemed to be claiming that I was her son to help me get out of the country I had a bad feeling in there and I got a voice in my head that was telling me get out of here now. I wasn't going to stick around so it took off and thought to myself I would rather take my chances with the Philadelphia Crips than the feds" I left and went to numerous hotels bordering the airport and couldn't get a hotel and some said I had to have a reservation, and one of them I seemed like I was black listed or labeled a terrorist so I went into what I thought was a big hotel it was some kind of housing and the security guy followed me out because I walked on the grass.
I hid in the bushes of a big hotel and waited for a while because I thought I had people after me and sat in the bushes and laid there for a hour or two. After that I walked to a Marriott (I think) and waited for a while because I was tired of walking around looking for a place to get some sleep so I waited until about six am and asked a younger black guy if I could get a ride to the airport and I got on a shuttle with a bunch of government people politician types and one guys wife said "it's because of you our country looks like shit" or something like that.

At the Airport it's seemed weird and I thought that the maintenance guys got smoked in the airport and I asked a guy that works there if someone died last night and he said "yeah." They seemed like they didn't want to sell me a ticket to Bismarck and were hassling me I had to call a number to get a partial refund on my ticket and I guy walked up to the ticket lady and said "sell him a ticket or the worlds going to end", it seemed like he was joking a bit.

So, I got a ticket and finally got on a plane to Bismarck it felt fairly chill. When I arrived in Bismarck I started walking out of the airport no ride in sight I walked down the road for quite a while I thought I would just walk to town I could hear nail guns going from some guys doing a roof and thought I could communicate through and sound impacting on the roof. When I was walking a car sent me a message if you're a psychic where is jimmy Hoffa buried, I asked some crickets they chirped Oakland stadium 7-8 feet down on 50-yard line. I ended up walking up to the college and there was some helicopter flying around and I took of my shirt and changed I believe I would change my clothes in the bathrooms when I thought people were following me I did this in the dc airport earlier. I asked a college kid for a ride and said he would give me one so I got in with him and asked for a ride to the greyhound he gave me a ride into Bismarck and I thanked him and asked him if he wanted some gas money (he turned it down) and I went on my way to the bus station.
In the bus station there was a black guy and a young white guy with a big duffle sack which he asked to trade for my green backpack and I traded him I think It was a bad trade and he ripped it putting his stuff in he told me his brother was a blood that killed a judge or something along

those lines and he was sad.

On the way to billings I had a bad vibe from the crew in the bus and an old man told me that I should try to listen in to Morris code. This was similar to an old guy that told me that Obama was in a secret underground fortress underneath the white house while I was taking the greyhound from Pittsburgh to D.C

While I was on the way to billings the guys behind me where being assholes I stood up for myself flipped them off and tried to scare them telepathically and it seemed to work. One guy got so scared he got off early and didn't get back on, or it was just his stop. I thought that I would get a warm reception in billings.

In Billings I went to the outlaw hotel and slept walked to the west end and checked to see if jade was at the holiday store, but I did not see her working. I tried to get into the crown plaza but it was booked and walked thru burn the point on the Northside and had strong signal powers and blasted them thru town and I thought I was sharing giving the crowds of people their own part of my powers and I swear a lot of people said thank you for the powers jeff. I went over to Lyles trailer and he gave me a tall can of Coors I said that he was replaced and I was the space police I took a sip of the beer and tossed it into a trash can when I walked out of his place abruptly and down the alley. Then I walked to where carter worked doc and eddies on the west end and asked if carter was around to Stan Doff he said he was in the back and I didn't go to the back. While I was sitting outside on the curb, I heard a car go by banging Big and Pac and it said on the cd that big Jeff should be getting head on every block. Seemed like the words might have been switched to that. I had visions of carter being picked up a UFO and taken to a mars concrete habitat where he would get water and food dispensed to him and had a fat alien girl that he had continual sex with. I walked back down central and over by Albertsons and rested and hid in a new construction house where a took a leak and rested in for a bit I was feeling a bit sick at the time.

I ended up getting a ride to Dillon with my dad at some point I am having problems remembering the time that this happened I had to have ride a bus to Bozeman. When I was in Dillon, I got a ticket at the smoke shop and took the bus down to Sacramento I thought I saw spike lee on the bus and Steve'o with big lumps on the sides of his forehead there was a black guy that had to be late 30's with a white woman about the same age I thought he was working with the police and was pretending to be from Philadelphia on the greyhound hung out in Sacramento first went to Oakland I thought I was psychic and I could help find missing women and children. I sat next to a pregnant black woman read her mind and realized I couldn't work with the police and blessed her, her boyfriend or husband was bothered.

I took a bus to the Oakland airport and realized I could fly to japan, but not until the next day so went back to the Sacramento bus stop and hung out all day talked to a hot black chick with a weave some guys were smoking a blunt and I didn't hit it and later noticed she had a ponch on her stomach and she hit a little Mexican dudes blunt. I hit on her and said she was to pretty to be out there by herself. While I was on the bus to Sacramento It stopped in Reno I thought I saw spike lee and his son and some signals told me that spike lee was in a police station saying I was a terrorist and was pretty weird. I don't know if he picked up on some of the signals coming out of me.

I walked to McDonalds in sac town before that I got ripped off at a Mexican restaurant they didn't give me my change and the owner seemed to have an attitude or a problem with me. Back at the bus stop an older prison style white guy showed up and he was mad that I'm not a racist; and later I heard an S.P.M song that seemed like he was talking shit. Some black guys showed up and thru signals I thought that they were friends with demon and the guys who jumped me. I could not stand hanging out at the bus station because I was picking up strange signals from the TV's in the bus station, I told the security guard I could not stand to be around the T.V. After a while on hanging out outside I got a ticket to the Portland.

On the way to Portland I thought I had some strange characters on the bus following me one of those people was a guy named mike S and I thought I made a power full statement that made his cock disappear. He was saying some strange stuff, I thought he was a rat. I also thought I saw my friend's sister on the way up there I think she said, "Sorry Jeff". When I got to Portland, I saw a Jamaican guy in a wheelchair, and he seemed cool. I sat down and go bit by a little beetle a nasty little sucker, some voices in my head said it was an Obama space beetle and that his space ship was full of them and counterfeit money, space cash. Then I walked through town trying to find a dock that would have a captain I could bribe to take me out to sea to another country. I walked I a direction I remembered to the river and got to a clinic and took a rest outside went to mall for some food I got some pizza and took a leak not very many bathrooms in businesses in Portland, I thought it seemed more dangerous for germs. Back to the clinic rested outside at that time I thought I had the cure for aids in my blood. I saw a coast guard helicopter with two contraptions on the sides kind of like two square bazookas. Started following the helicopters path to the docks I saw a submarine and a big ship being constructed.

I got some pizza next to a park and kept walking to the docks went by a beer fest that crossed a segmented overlay bridge. Took a rest on the other side by the road. I thought I heard them talking about me on the radio at the park. I kept walking asked directions from a guy older are walked down a big hill until I got to a convenience store then headed down the road past some city trams, past some city buses past jail's and treatment centers until I got to the docks then laid down until I walked up to a security check booth and asked about boarding ships he said that they were just doing work on secret navy ships(I thought it was frequency antennas') I also thought he got a hundred bucks to tell me that.
Then I started walking back got by a truck depot and heard a high pitch noise thought that they had activated the equipment on the ship that was getting worked on in a warehouse by the

security booth were they were doing some welding on it. Started walking up a hill stopped before the dock and thought I was psychic messing with the presidents speck I could hear coming from the building's jails treatment center and such. I sent signals to necro and told him to write cleaner raps and talked to him about not being so focused on bad things. On the way up the hill I stopped and god said go ahead take a dump and the mixed nuts I ate were messing with my stomach so I walked up the stairs and took a big runny dump and wiped my butt with a sock and left it, It was on the side of the road and late at night. Also made a power statement that I wanted shit to be smeared on the faces of the evil people in congress- or the government. Me and the lord had a hearty laugh!

I walked up the hill and found a hotel managed by an Indian man and his wife. I rented a room and slept next door to some skate boarders. I kept telling people that if you have advanced aids you must use condoms or you soul will be sent to hell. I thought Portland had a 25 percent dropple ganger infestation. That should jump into the ocean or a river and feed Gaia's beast sharks and the fish if they have the advanced aids. I woke up and had a signal talk with big ben said he never raped that collage girl. Everyone at the hotel could see my visions of Eskimo girls when I was jacking off, I thought and felt bad I thought his wife knew the inn keepers. I got up and walked down the road. Walking in a parched parked with brown grass I made a power statement to bring the crickets back and to make the grass greener in Portland. I thought I heard some ghost crickets.

Later on while I was walking I saw a man thought I was homeless and he seemed to be in some tough times himself had lots of track marks asked questions about god he talked of molecules in tress and I talked of Gods and devils I argued with him for a bit and blessed him and left shook his hand.

Then I went to the train stop gave a bad look to a black built guy talking to a white cute girl think she kept mentioning because my thoughts were going on the teleprompters. Also had brought up to people Facebook is the Necronomicon and the two Zuckerberg's are evil space aliens w/ evil smart technology. The built black dude was cool later on, on the train and I went back to the grey hound had to ask directions and went to Spokane.

In Spokane at a bus stop I saw a possible fed go upstairs and through signals I thought he raped a women walking home from a bar.

After a while I went downtown Spokane went down the street went to the store and bought a Newcastle and a bag of yogurt pretzels sat on a stoop and ate them and drank my beers, had a signal about all the previous me's that had died trying to get this far and said I hadn't made it the farthest yet went down to a bar and had a beer and left a signal said it was poisoned and that it cured the bug bite I got in Portland that would of gave me aids. Walked to a parking lot and took a piss between buildings went and got some soul food at a barbeque place that an older black guy owned and had his daughter hanging out there with him it seemed. I ate a 10 dollar chicken meal and left got some racist signals from him went and relaxed on the grass and saw a truck with Washington plates I thought was D.C and I thought they were there to kill me so I left went back to the bus stop eventually had some homeless black guy say some nice things about me like that he thought I was Jesus and threw his beer in a trash can there was some cops around and It was day time. I was upstairs and I thought I heard some signals about a maintenance man that he was pedophilia when he was a kid, and he took off out the door. Then I saw a bald head guy that had just gotten out of prison with his mom, his brother and his sister. I thought he was a cleanup guy for a white power gang in prison. I thought about throwing him over a stairwell he was a prick. Then the bus came his mom stayed there and he followed his bro and sis to Missoula. I knew that he a prison group guy when he kept saying if I had my knifes. He kept stealing kisses from a girl in a seat behind him. I finally said, "Hey is he bothering you?" she didn't say anything I said, "speak up if he is!' She said "I don't know" her boyfriend or brother was a pussy who would not say anything I yelled across the bus "leave her alone ".

At our stop in Missoula his family or friends that were with him said he said what do you expect just got out of prison. In Missoula I thought they were getting off. The bus driver said to him you do that again and you'll get a sexual assault. They got on the bus as me again going to butte and I thought I saw a pyramid space ship. I made a power statement about his friend's guns to melt that I thought were going to set me up in billings. Made a power statement about the guns melting and the white con said his friends arm melted off and a sniped rifle melted, and all their guns melted he said you don't know how much those guns cost. Made a power statement that his feet would burn. They got off the bus in butte and I continued to Bozeman.

I ended up getting a hotel room at the Rim view at this time I believe and crashed hard had visions or reptilian aliens that were horny and a lizard alien planet when earthling men would go and get their junk eaten by the reptilian sexual organs. I spent so hard that I woke up to a wakeup call from the hotel asking if I was paying for another night, I think I did. I saw the hotel cleaning staff sitting outside acting scared and strange noises coming from the cars driving by, frequency's coming from the tire friction on the road. That evening I went on the road next to Lyle's trailer sat on the curb for a bit and sat there and a cop slowly drove by me. I went to Lyle's trailer and the voices in my head told me that Lyle was dead and that someone else was living in his house that was involved with killing him, so I wrapped my shirt around my hands and kicked in his door. He yelled get the fuck out of here I said "hey Lyle" and he said "hey for a minute," and then "get the fuck out of here!" I tried to leave but the door was stuck and I couldn't get out he was yelling, I finally got it open and left for a while I came back in the morning when he went to work and kept kicking his door in I saw a brown suit case full of personal papers in the living room and grabbed them along with my shirt that I had left the first time I kicked the door in.

I'm pretty sure I went to the gray hound station after that I saw a couple I young white guy like myself and his women he made some comment about me staring at them. I used mental telekinesis and made the young guy say "I like to eat dog food" multiple times after he said that he was surprised and was going "What the hell is going on?" I firmly believed in dropple gangers at that time and thought the bus stop was full of them. I also mentally told him that his women had aids he told her to get a blood test and got on their bus. At the grey hound station I saw a black guy that I recognized from Pittsburg I asked him what he was doing there and he told me that he was traveling to California to visit some friends or family, we later got into it when he told me that I stunk, I told him I would body slam his little munchkin ass, he said good job sticking up for yourself.

I ended up taking a bus to Bozeman and walked from the old bus stop in Bozeman to four corners which is quite a distance, I would telekinetically try to get people to fight me that where driving by I also was trying to hit on women driving by with my mind one I thought said meet me at five at Mc Donald's and bring condoms. I think I was just tripping out at this time in hindsight.

 I was trying to communicate with my friend ray with telekinesis to get him to pick me up at the corner club which didn't work. I started walking south of four corners to where I thought his house was or my brother lived down the road in elk grove and I was very lucky and my brother was driving by and saw me and picked me up walking when I was walking down the street over by four corners. My brother was surprised to see me walking and gave me a ride to my parents' house that I didn't know where it was. I ended up sleeping for a while but I was used to traveling so I walked to Belgrade on foot I had scared my mom by saying I was going to walk to Bozeman cat's paw and fight some people so while I was walked down jackrabbit the cop's rolled up on me they asked what I was doing and said my mom told them that I had a gun. Which I didn't they took me to hope house in Bozeman and they did a psychiatric evaluation and they couldn't commit me so I walked to a hotel close by rented a room and got some sleep I could hear two brothers talking about me in a room below me. At this point I got a bus to billings. I got sketched out on the bus to billing and got out in laurel at this point I walked to park city tried to get a hotel but no vacancy's so I walked back to laurel next to the train tracks and almost got hit in the head by the bars on the sides of the train. I was hoping a UFO would pick me up and take me to another country like china or japan. On a dirt road over by the train tracks I thought I saw a U.F.O. that look like a DeLorean with a bar on lights on the front kind on sparkling light pattern going from- one side to the other on the front grill. It swooped down by me on the dirt road. Saw a blue orb at the train tracks and thought about how I wanted to get picked up, I had a signal that an army guy got fried by radiation trying to board a blue orb like the one's I was trying to get on while I was hanging out by the train tracks near Laurel Montana. I was having visons of dead beings like Karthus (skeleton pope creatures)(who is also a League of Legends character flying UFOs then I walked to Billings from Laurel and when I got to billings I went to 27th street of the highway. I think I got a hotel at the Rimview Motel. I went to target and got a brief case and met my daughter at Fuddruckers with her and my parents and I got a big bag at target to carry my stuff clothes and stuff when I walked to the Lewis and Clark and got a hotel room and stayed for a while could hear the neighboring rooms talking and thought one of the neighbor rooms were haunted so I got my hatchet out held it by my side and was walking around the rooms and spray painted a white cross on the door and put it away because

I knew the cops were called when the hotel owner was pissed I painted the door. I said I would pay for the door and I went into my room and put my hatchet in a drawer and put my hands up when the cops rolled up. Took me to the billings clinic and they put me in a wheel chair and wheeled a long way, like I was Hannibal Lecter or something to a room in a locked hall way with a small T.V room at the end. And saw a ghost in the hall way and some weird people there a Mexican and a fat white dude from Illinois that I thought was from a satanic cult. This Mexican or Indian guy from the southside that was in the same living block was saying one morning that Jesus' raped me last night. I had a beard I told him to shut up. I could also seem to throw voices around in the office type area behind the locked hallway door. I was there for about a week. I had saw a vision or hallucination of my dead friend looking in my room window. Before I left I had about 2,000 dollars in a envelope that was the last of my savings from working and some desk clerk lady had it stashed under her key board. And they found it under her keyboard, what a fucking bitch.

The food wasn't too bad but the living quarters sucked, and this Indian (from India) doctor had it in for me after the axe incident.

 The court transportation cop took me to the courthouse in when I was getting in the elevator, I saw my buddy randy when I had my wrist shackled, I was like "what's up dude". I do not know if he recognized me, but he did not say anything. Russal fagg was my judge and he sentenced me to my second commitment in warm springs. I was stupidly pissed off at him because he let the Satanist from Chicago go and I had to go to a 3-month commitment to warm springs. (which isn't too bad considering. "I yelled; shit your letting him go and this is my hometown" my public defender didn't want me to say anything, but I told my side off the story. And I was off the warm springs for the second time. I was transported from billings clinic to warm spring in the back off a cop car, the cop let me out in Bozeman at the gas station at griffin to stretch my legs. And drove me the rest of the way to warm springs. The took me into the booking part and I went back in for around another 3-months. I was inside with some new people, I heard voices coming from the floor and when I pounded on the floor in the unit A, it sounded empty, I told them that it sounded hollow I wondered if they had put people under the unit and the died and rotten into skeletons down there. And they had a big vacuum tube sucking up everything up and a cleaning crew cleaning the hollow part. I could hear them sucking stuff up (what I still think may be remanence of dead people under the floor in a hidden- basement floor. I could hear the voices of my old friend's, Matt and Jon under the ground that's what made me tripped me out. There was a big white dude I called a fake pimp because he was accused of pimping some girl out. I yelled at that guy for walking into my room at night I said, "I would fuck up the next person that walked into my room". I worked on models an F15 airplane maybe another one I have forgotten about?
 I stopped a crazy girl from destroying the T.V but not the case around it. It was funny to me to watch the case break. I worked washing dishes for minimum wage again. I this dude kind of fat with tattoos that was jealous of my reputation worked in the video booth instead of the kitchen

like the last time I was in there for my first commitment. We would try to play risk with a few younger guys. One of them was charged with robbing a store pretty sure he was awaiting trial. I smoked some Tobacco and it got me high because I hadn't smoked in a while. I thought I would have to stay longer if they smelled tobacco on me. I would lift weights and play basketball in my free time. I would have all kinds of food in my room granola bars and stuff from the little store there and some stuff that my parents brought me. A bearded guy I think his name was Arron, tried to get out and smashed through some doors. This dude Charles was a trip he would smash windows because he liked the sound of them breaking. And this guy that thought he was super women I almost beat him up for talking shit. I also wrote down I bunch of notes that helped me write this story. I do not remember too much about my second commitment might be because I smoked too much weed, or I gave myself brain damage by sleep deprivation.

I've been watching sprit box videos and I think I can similarly contact aliens or spirits though electronic appliances' fridges, fans. I think the show the path took some of my T.V problems from my bus stations in Sacramento and D.C when the T.V told me to kill myself in D.C and noise problems in Sacramento bus station with the T.V's, Now shows like legion and Jeff & the aliens are coming on TV

It seems like I can hear for miles and miles like the song says and I can always hear when people talk about me.

I swear that show legion stole some of my idea's here is an idea I wrote down before I ever saw legion. Here is an idea I wrote down before the show ever aired. A mental patient goes off his meds and his powers start coming back hearing things people talking about him frequencies and audible small voices – and static clouds hovering over people's houses in the neighborhood.

A bunch off rappers start rapping about jeffboz and talking about spaceships and aliens and wanting to leave earth.

Post Malone was wearing a yellow don't tread on me shirt on one of the pictures on the show hot ones. The same one on the flag of the Oregon right wing government building occupiers. And the same one I was wearing 5 or 6 years ago in the D.C. airport.

My ears get hot or start buzzing sometimes.

A bunch of people start listening to a normal guys Pandora and playing the music he listens too.

Another idea of mine is a funny poltergeist movie with a stoner guy getting haunted and he doesn't care about it because he is high all the time.

Some of the strange dreams I've had go as follows; I had a dream I was in a court or school something like that and saw the sky fill with light coming in as sections like a pie or pizza cuts with blue light coming out of them. Then a big UFO came in with a big ruckus blasted in and landed a big cargo ship look like a giant box style harrier plane and I starting running and woke up.

That's all for now about me and my idea's, thank you for reading my story and a few of my thoughts and dreams and experiences.

Jeff Bozorth wrote this my contact info is (removed) There are also some famous rappers shouting me out.

 I think THC can make it easier to hear frequencies that are alien in nature or from outer space Lcd or mushrooms might have the same effects for some people. Lately I have just been cleaning up horse crap and cleaning horse hooves every day and COVID-19 19 is killing a lot of people. I have been playing video games cooking food and spending time with family I just went grocery shopping today with my daughter. The new Xbox and PlayStation are coming out and I don't think I will get one for a while I will keep on trying to defeat the backlog of games I have before I get a new system.

 I think if you do not sleep for days or weeks you can start hearing supernatural stuff and seeing other worldly objects in the sky.

Joe Biden just got elected president. I used to upload game videos on YouTube but the software started messing up so I could not do that anymore. Been baking and cooking dinner for family and reading fantasy adventure novels in my spare time. Recreational marijuana just passed in Montana so they will be taxing and making income for the state off it. I was writing my friend in prison and drawing him pictures he caught COVID-19 and got over it, thankfully.

I am reminded of Chong from Cheech and Chong saying "Hey Man, I am my own best customer" I feel that way if I end up with weed because I do not sell it. Still playing video games and spending time with family buying presents for nieces and nephews doing the same old same old. Staying out of trouble gave up drinking for at least 2 or 3 years cause I do dumb stuff like climb chain link fences and slice open my hand where my friend ike said man that looks like a vagina because of the big hole sliced in the side of my hand that was bleeding all over the place and I drove myself to the urgent care where they stitched my had up and a cop had me take a cab to four corners there my mom picked me up when I was walking down jackrabbit.

The THC frequency hearing through sound waves with marijuana hearing another universe or places, people or locations through electronics and or possibility or radio or micro waves, or could just be signals from space that gets hacked from time to time with false broadcasts and if you move your mouth when you are hearing them some people could trip out on you or think your mental unless they had the inside scoop. Jeff is like a cell phone tower for aliens when he gets high some different races of aliens or beings can communicate for long distances In his constant hiss of changing sound waves.

 A man that has been made strong mentally by people or bad sprits or demons messing with him all the time and they use his mind for audible conversations but when you try to record them they go away.

The signal is moving locations and seems to emit when I am looking at the computer screen towards my left ear and goes away when I look way or towards it like sense I stopped using my small fan it seems to come from the stove now.

Here is an Idea a schizophrenic guy with special powers gets enhanced meds from the government in his vials that they are experimenting on him with CIA chemicals.

Here is another idea for a sci fi story a guy is pregnant with a demon that gives him strength it always just looks kind of like a beer belly, another is a guy that can't hear people talk very well so he figures out how to hear differently and listen to sounds and the word sounds it makes and can make sense of beeping and sound notes some sort of morse code a guy that is very influential and people like the music he likes and listens to on YouTube.

A story about a kid who is working outside and sees strange worm creatures in the horse poop in the wheel barrel then he is standing in a big water puddle-pond and the creature a giant one comes up from underneath him and devours him in two to three big bites.

A space station with a dude playing video games growing weed and chilling with chicks, a guy grows a weed plant that turns into a women until he harvests then she gets murdered but he really killed her because he killed the plant.

An alien that breaks his friend out of jail wearing an mask they think but it is his real face because he is really an alien.

Hearing frequencies becoming a conduit for transmissions or sound wave frequencies and being able to affect it with our own brain waves or strong thoughts and hold discussions with different signal or be harassed by the evil or corrupted signals, ones that taunt you and say things that would bother a normal person. And starting to play video games or leave and do something else to avoid the corrupted signals.

Possibly being able to transmit your thoughts on the teleprompter on the t.v so people on t.v sets can see your thoughts.

A guy kind of an outcast gets notices by aliens because of the songs he plays he DJ's to the aliens the songs he likes. I think in stead of selling aliens nukes and guns we should sell them weed, mushrooms and video games.

As far as getting signal jeff is like a tuning fork to fine tune the messages, what if the aliens had a big laser gun like a Nazi rail gun and If some one on earth made them mad they could just blast them with their big laser cannon instantaneously. Everyone on earth would look at the smoldering spot and wonder what just happened to the fella standing there.

This has been some thoughts from Jeff Bozorth A guy from Billings, Bozeman, Dillion, Idaho falls and Roseburg Oregon. Studying the way that foreign sounds hit the ear resulting in interpreting the beeps or signal and translating them into words.

I would like to thank my parents Tim and Denise my daughter Bianca and my brother Ben and his family Rita and the kids.